WINGLESS!

A FAIRLY WEIRD FAIRY TALE

WINGLESS
A FAIRLY WEIRD FAIRY TALE

BY
PARO ANAND
WITH EQUALLY WEIRD ILLUSTRATIONS BY
ATANU ROY

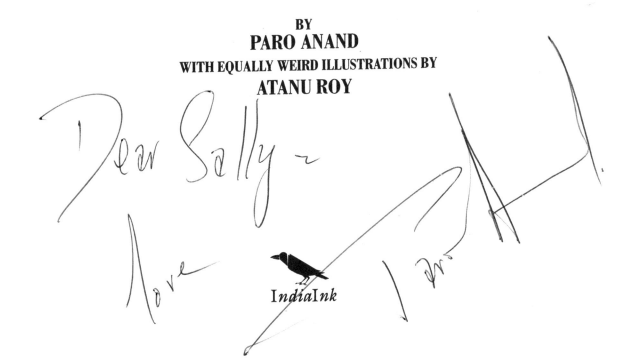

Dear Sally ~
love

IndiaInk

IndiaInk

First published by IndiaInk, 2003
Fourth impression, 2017

IndiaInk
An imprint of
Roli Books Pvt. Ltd.
M-75, Greater Kailash-II Market
New Delhi-110048
Phone: ++91-11-40682000
Email: info@rolibooks.com
Website: www.rolibooks.com

Also at
Bangalore, Chennai & Mumbai

ISBN: 978-81-86939-16-1

Designed by Atanu Roy

Printed and bound at Nutech Print Services - India

To those who teach me
everyday that it's
possible to fly
wingless–

Aditi and Uday
Shiv and Gautam
Viraj and Sanya
And, as always, Keshav

– Paro

To Varsha for 'cooking' up all
those cr-edible excuses
for my publishers while I
generally slept on the job.

To most of my friends and
relatives who still remain
blissfully unaware as to
what I do for a living.

To all fun-loving kids
everywhere.

– Atanu

Paro Anand loves to write for, work with and play with children. She's an award-winning writer, an editor, and runs a program called 'Literature in Action'. This is her 10th book for children. And there are more on the way.

Atanu Roy has illustrated more than a hundred books for children in various styles. He is also a cartoonist and a designer. He holds workshops on book illustration and cartooning all over the country for schools and organisations.

CONTENTSSSSSS....

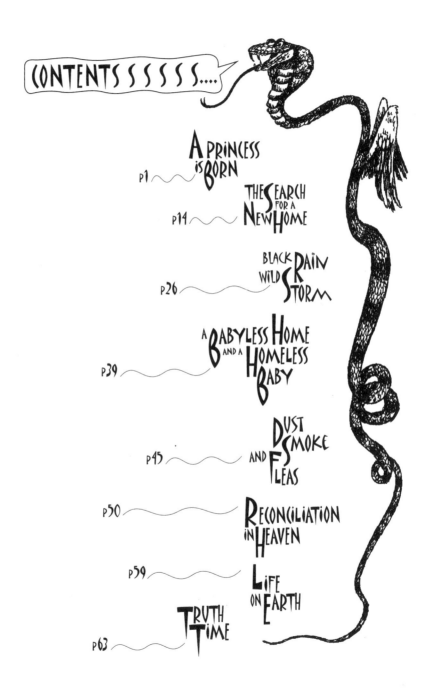

A PRINCESS is BORN

WHEN Princess Chutki was born to the King and Queen of Angels, there should have been much rejoicing and happiness. There should have been music, festivals, feasts and gifts. There should have been a smile on the face of anyone who lived in the silver and diamond land of the Angels where King Quicksilver and Queen Sparkling Gem ruled justly and wisely. Just as any good King and Queen should, in any good fairy tale. There should have been all of this. Or at least some of it.

But there wasn't. Not any of these joyful things happened. No. The musical instruments were broken, festivals banned, the feasts that cooks had been preparing for weeks were thrown to dogs and cats, crows and worms. Gifts wrapped and ready for the new princess were hidden away into the darkest corners for spiders to spin their webs around and for dust to settle on. The smiles on the faces of everyone who lived in the land of the Angels turned to frowns, or even tears. Real watery, salty tears, not the tiny diamonds that angels are supposed to weep on the few occasions when angels weep.

And those who wept the hardest of all were King Quicksilver and Queen Sparkling Gem. They had so looked forward to this baby angel and hoped she would be everything that a good and perfect angel should be.

And she was perfect. Well, almost. But not perfect enough. Not really good enough to be the princess of angels. No. Not at all.

The people who came to see her, opened their eyes wide with horror as their jaws fell with loud thuds to the floor. Some were speechless and hurried wordlessly away. Others could only weep and wash the floor with their tears as they fled from the horrible sight. Still others had tongues that would not stop wagging.

"The King and Queen must have done something VERY bad to deserve a daughter like this."

"The Kingdom of Angels is doomed. The end is in sight."

"We must kill this freakish princess before she kills us."

"She has brought Hell into Heaven. She must be punished."

As the news spread like wildfire and people started to gather at the palace gates, the King and Queen took the baby in her crib and moved to the highest room in the highest tower and ordered that all the gates and doors be locked securely. As the news

spread like wildfire, the wagging tongues grew louder and louder till all the kingdom was one big shout. Peace was shattered. Even the diamond domes of the palaces were cracking and tumbling down as the shouting grew to a fevered and maddening pitch. And the angels of the land shouted in one voice –

"KILL HER! KILL HER !! KILL HER !!!"

The King's face grew grey with worry.

The Queen's face grew white with fear.

But the shouting would not stop. It became so hot and angry that the silver streets melted, turning into liquid. And yet the angry angels swam about in the silver rivers and shouted and splashed and demanded that the newborn Princess Chutki must be killed.

King Quicksilver just did not know what to do.

"I just do not know what to do!" he said to his Queen who was now as white as a page on which not a word has been written.

The Queen said in a voice watery with tears, "Let's ask Nani Ma. After all, she's a thousand and three years old. Perhaps she has seen something like this before and knows what it means and what to do about it."

11

So Nani Ma was called. She was completely deaf, you see, being a thousand and three years old, and so she had not heard the wagging tongues and shouting voices. She only saw, with amazement, the people splashing about in silver streams instead of walking about on silver streets.

"Must be some kind of mad new passion or fashion," she muttered to herself. She had seen passions for fashions come and go, and had never liked a single one. No. Not these latest crazes in clothes, hair, buildings or behaviour.

She stuck to the fashions of a thousand years ago when women who were women wore sea-green seaweed gowns. These she still wore, keeping them fresh in underwater cupboards. Now she splashed through the rivers of silver and came to the palace door. She was shown into the bedroom where K. Quicksilver and Q. Sparkling Gem sat sadly on either side of the baby's crib.

"Oh!" she cried, as she saw the baby in bed, "why, how wonderful, Quickgem and Sparkling Silver, (she could never, ever, get their names right, not even her own daughter's!) You've had a baby. What darlings, how good of you to call me!"

She rushed to the baby's bedside and peered, "why, how beautiful, how perfect, what a good, little baby angel," she cooed as she lifted the little princess into her old and withered arms. But as she lifted her off the sheets and pillows, she suddenly let out a cry of alarm and dropped the little baby rudely back into the bed.

"Oh! Oh! OH!!" She shrieked in horror, "but what is this? This little baby has no wings! What's the use of an angel without wings? What is the meaning of this?"

Her hands fluttered all around like restless butterflies, resting here or there for a moment or two, before setting off again.

"What is the meaning of this, Sparking Gent?"

"Actually, we wanted to ask YOU the meaning of this," said the Queen in a voice loud enough to be rude to anyone but the Hard of Hearing. But the thousand and three year old Nani Ma could not, or would not hear.

"Why, Quick Slipper and Sprinkling Gent," she shouted in a shaky voice, "I say that you are doomed!" Then, in a voice now edged with black lace, as is proper when speaking of Bad Things, she continued, "You are doomed for having brought Hell to Heaven. What you have done, Quack Slicker and Cackling Hen, no one has dared to do before!! Only sorrow and tears will be your companions now…" and with a loud moan like wind on a moonless night, she swept out of the palace leaving only the fishy smell of old seaweed behind her.

"Quack Slicker, oh, I mean, Quicksilver, what are we going to do?" asked the Queen in fear.

"I don't know, Cackling Hen, I just don't know," sobbed the King. He didn't even realize what he had just called his wife.

Through all of this, I may add, Princess Chutki smiled and laughed and giggled. A most sweet smile, a lilting laugh and girlish giggle, such as a fairy tale princess must have. Her mother watched her little wingless baby with love and fear for her future, but the baby only smiled back, a smile as pure as a sparkling gem.

"Let's call Dadi Ma," suggested the King.
"If Nani Ma hasn't seen anything like this in a thousand and three

years, perhaps Dadi Ma has. After all, she's two thousand years and 364 days old."

And so, even as the shouting from outside grew louder and still louder, Dadi Ma was sent for. Now Dadi Ma, being almost a whole thousand years older that Nani Ma, could neither see nor hear, so she merely swam (she was a great swimmer, in spite of her great age). She effortlessly swam the distance between her house and the palace, without a hint of all the unrest that swam about her. She swam the crawl, breaststroke, butterfly and backstroke in a swift and unbroken medley race with herself. Her long hair flowed like serpents all around her in the silver stream. She wore her hair long, which was just as well, for she wore nothing else. And so she looked quite a sight as she emerged, all dripping silver and flowing hair, creating shiny puddles as she strode, unseeing and unhearing, to stand before the baby's crib. The weeping parents led Dadi Ma to the bed and put her hands on the baby.

"A Baby!" boomed the lady in a voice that shook the already cracking and crumbling domes, "why son, well done!" she said, slapping the delicate Queen hard on her back.

This sent the poor Queen into a long and lasting coughing fit, but Dadi Ma didn't notice as she grabbed the baby, bottom side up, into her arms.

She felt the baby's smooth and new bottom lovingly. "My what a beautiful smooth face the baby has," she boomed, "but for goodness sakes, where are it's eyes, nose and mouth? Heaven forbid, it doesn't even have ears!" All the same, she pinched the bottom's cheeks, which made the good Princess Chutki squeal and giggle and feel tickled pink.

The King and Queen managed to smile for the first time since their baby was born. Quicksilver quickly turned the baby right side up, so the grandmother could examine her more correctly.

"Oh!" said Dadi Ma, embarrassed, realizing her mistake, "thank you, my sweet daughter-in-law," and she kissed the king on both his cheeks, then mumbled, "my, how rough your face has become, daughter-in-law, don't tell me that you've taken to shaving?"

The King hurriedly withdrew his face and let the old lady examine the child right side up. Sure enough, soon, she too let out a bellow, like an enraged bull. "Look here, there's something missing. Do you realize that this is an angel baby without wings? Do you realize that angels must always, but always, have babies with wings, son?" And here she caught hold of the Queen's ear and shook her so vigorously that she was soon flying about, with only her ear attached to her mother-in-law's hand.

Finally Dadi Ma let the ear go and let the Queen fall in a heap onto the floor. Dadi Ma, in stepping over her, tripped and fell. "Oh, what is this bundle of dhobi clothes doing in the middle of the floor? Really, daughter-in-law, you just don't know how to live like a queen!" And here she poked her son in his eye, then felt his cheeks again.

"Really, what is Heaven coming to? Angels without wings and Queens who shave their faces. Here, catch..." she boomed, as she flung the baby

back to her parents and then took a superb swallow-dive from out of the window.

Unfortunately, the angry people had got quite hungry and had gone home for dinner. The liquid silver river had turned back into a solid silver street once again. CRUNCH! went the old lady as she hit the street far down below. Fortunately, her long, flowing and thick hair saved her and broke her fall, instead of her bones. She got up, dusted the silver dust off herself, and marched off muttering, "Angels without wings, women who shave their faces, and dhobi clothes in the middle of palaces, streets that become rivers and rivers that become streets. Tsk! Tsk! What next? What next?"

Well what's next was that the people, having had their dinners, felt quite sleepy, which was only natural if you think of all the shouting and swimming they had done all day long. So they decided that they would turn in for the night and try to kill the wingless princess the next day.

For the king and queen though, as you can imagine, there was no rest or sleep, or even dinner. They sat in worried thought and watched their happy baby unhappily.

One shadow lurked amongst the crowd. He listened quietly to what everyone had to say. He even shouted, "We must kill her!" along with the other maddened angels. But as soon as all was quiet, he slipped unseen into the palace. Here, at the door of the highest room of the highest tower, he knocked.

"Whoever you are, go away!" commanded the King.

"It is I, old Zamroo of Zamroodpur, I must talk to you."

"How can we be sure that you mean our baby no harm?"

"One thousand years ago, when I was born with 'W'-shaped wings instead of the standard 'V'-shaped ones, your father, the King prevented the angels from cutting my wings off. He convinced the angels that W was a wery write shape. For, after all, you write Wings with a 'W'. They are Wings not Vings. That perhaps, this was the shape of wings to come. Of course he was just being very wise and witty, but through all this, the angels learned that they should try to understand someone or something which is different from them. Just because a person is not EXACTLY like you, does not mean that he is not a person. It just means that he's a person who has some things or some wings that are different from you and other things that are the same." He stopped to catch his breath for he was not used to making such long speeches. Then, shaking his head sadly, he said, "But, obviously, they didn't learn this lesson well enough...

"Anyway, since then, I have always been a good and loyal servant of the royal house. I would give my very life before allowing a single hair of the little princess to be harmed."

So the King and Queen opened the door and let old Zamroo of Zamroodpur in. With tears in his eyes, as he looked upon the infant as she lay in smiling sleep, he told the royals the wicked plans of the angels. "They have sworn to kill her in the morning," he wept. "How wicked are those who seem to be so good...

"They will kill her, you know," he said.

"What angels are these, who have no compassion or love or pity for a helpless newborn baby?" said the queen.

"But a baby without wings, don't you see?" said the King.

"Of course I see, but that's through no fault of hers. Look at Nakubhai Nakdil, he was born with such a long nose, but no one wants to kill him for it. Or... or Begum Baihaath, who was born with two left hands and no right. And think of Mia Ganjoodin, whose head has always been as smooth as a newborn baby's bottom, with never a single hair sprouting! What right have these to live in peace amongst angels, and not our one and only daughter for having no wings? That shouldn't change anything," she said. "Yes, only everything," sighed Zamroo.

"I know, Queen, but, you see, don't you, that an angel without wings is just... is just a human being. Then how can she live and rule Angel Land?"

BeGum BAIHaaTh

The King and Queen sat in troubled thought. And Zamroo sat with them. Then the King finally spoke, in a voice heavy with tiredness and sorrow.

"If our little girl looks like a human being, perhaps that's the best place for her to be."

"Where?"

"On earth, among people."

"She's our daughter! How can you be so cruel as to think of giving her away?"

Mia Ganjoodin

"Would it be less cruel to allow the mad mob to kill her tomorrow morning?"

NakHubhai NakdiL

After a long, long pause, the Queen nodded her head, "Yes, I fear you are right Quicksilver, there seems to be no other way… We will take her to earth."

"I will go with you," said Zamroo.

So, without further delay, the King and Queen of Angels put on their darkest, drabbest clothes and wrapped their baby in a warm shawl. Then, under cover of the dark, moonless night, the three royals and their loyal servant caught the nearest shooting star and sped rapidly to earth.

THE SEARCH FOR A NEW HOME

ON the way down, the parents held the baby, turn by turn. Close to their hearts. Close to tears. They discussed their plans.

"We must choose our baby's new home with great care."

"To make sure of that, no effort we'll spare."

"The house should be so big and fine."

"With diamonds and silver, as is mine."

"Children to play with would be fun."

"And to sleep together when the day is done."

"And she must have lots to eat."

"Some of salt and some of sweet."

"Some Roohafza to wash it down."

"On her head should sparkle a diamond crown."

"Ah! There's a house all stuffed with wealth."

"To look after our baby, through sickness and health."

And so it was that King QS and Queen SG landed in the beautiful gardens of Seth Neela Note's estate. Fountains splashed to the latest filmi tunes and prize dahlias stood in straight lines like policemen

14

on parade. The angels crept up the grand stairs upto the huge, carved front door. Now you may wonder how they're all going to get in, but remember, they're angels, so no big carved door is going to keep them out. They just vaporized themselves, became thin air (even though Queen SG was a bit on the plump side) and whiffed themselves, baby and all, through the keyhole.

Although they couldn't be seen, they could be smelled. Although they smelled good, they smelled otherworldly, strange. Although the dogs were small white Pomeranians, they had very sharp noses and very shrill barks. Although Seth Neela Note and Mrs. Note snored loudly as they slept soundly on their soft white beds, the Poms barked much louder. And although Seth and Mrs. Note were very sound sleepers, the sound of six yapping Poms woke them up. Now, although the dogs could smell the angels in the house, the human beings could not see them anywhere. So, although they had kept the dogs as guard dogs, they now kicked them in the ribs and told them to "shut up and let us sleep!"

By this time the children had got up too and, not knowing what was going on,

they kicked the dogs some more before jumping right back into their soft, white beds.

The King and Queen had not liked what they had seen. But they decided to wait till morning to see if the Note family behaved better in the sunshine. Luckily, there were some nice, soft, white beds spare, so finally, the tired royals slept. This time the poor Poms didn't sleep. Their nostrils tingled with exciting and strange smells, but the pain in their ribs reminded them to keep their thoughts and noses to themselves.

In the morning, the angels awoke to the most unpleasant sounds that they had ever heard. Like, the sound of the bell ringing for the start of a double math's period. Only worse. Like the sound of the alarm clock, when you want to sleep some more. Only even worse. Something like the sound of loud crashing when you've just broken your mother's favourite and most expensive crystal vase. Only much, much worse. Even if you can't begin to imagine anything worse than that.

They opened their eyes to flashing lights and screams and yells of the most awful kind. And worst of all, there was someone shouting, "KILLKILLKILL!" Quick as a flash, all the three adult angels leapt onto the baby angel in order to protect her. They all thought that the angry angels had discovered them and were now determined to complete their dirty work.

Princess Chutki squealed herself awake. There were too many angels on top of her to allow her to sleep comfortably. The older angels looked around in panic, but could see none of the angry mob about. But the flashing and yelling still continued.

Old Zamroo said that he would take a look around while the parents stayed with the baby. Soon, in fact immediately, he was back. "I think the princess is safe for now, but you can't imagine what the children are up to. Come and look…"

The three Note children, Bada Note, Chotta Note and Change, sat in front of a flashing screen. Men and animals leapt about the screen. The two bigger children sat with a panel of buttons in front of them. The youngest shouted KILLKILLKILL! And, by pressing buttons on their panels, the children would make the screen-men fire guns, which

duly killed the running animals. Every time an animal fell, it would yelp out, and the children would yell in happiness.

All of this did not look good to the angels. "This is not a good home for our baby," they said, "we must find another." The dogs whined and fretted as the angels made for the door and let themselves out of the keyhole.

"If rich families are like this, perhaps we should choose a poor family," the angels thought, and so they made their way to a broken down part of town. Runny-nosed children scratched their heads and gaped in open-mouthed half-curiosity at the three new-comers with a bundle of baby. But the Queen's smiley smile beamed a little bit of happiness and hope into their sad hearts and made them glad, even if for a little moment of time. None of the angels spoke. Each one was dreading having to leave their precious load here amidst the filth and sadness that hung like a gray beast over the slum, sucking up the watery sun with its huge mouth.

They peeped into every broken hut. Some children were sick. Others hungry, some lonely, some just crying because that's what they were used to doing. But others too were giggling, enjoying some secret childhood game, dancing to silent tunes.

"What do you think?" asked King Quicksilver.

"I - I don't know…" replied Queen Sparkling Gem helplessly, hopelessly, miserably.

"Think?" snapped Zamroo, impatiently taking the baby into his own old arms. "There's nothing to think. No matter what, this is no fit place for our princess. She could never survive all this hunger and dirt. We may as well

just kill her off right now ourselves, and save her the troubles that are bound to follow."

Both parents were relieved by the old angel's decisive voice. Yes, of course, they couldn't leave their little daughter here, no matter what. So they made their way back, through the oily, splashless water-filled street. Back past every holey home. It made the Queen weep to see such poverty. Which was just as well – her weeping I mean – because the Queen wept diamond and pearl tears that bounced onto the road and rolled to the feet of the snot-nosed children. They gathered the moon-shiny beads and ran to show their parents. And, as you can imagine, they weren't so poor after that. But this the angels never knew, for they were already on their way.

"Not too rich and not too poor," thought the parents, gliding along the pavement, holding their baby. As they passed a park, they saw a group of six girls, all dressed alike. There were playing. Their parents sat on a bench close by. The mother's tummy was round and big. She would have a seventh baby soon.

The Queen smiled happily. "My baby will be most happy with so many lovely sisters," she said and was about to put Chutki down near the parents. But then she heard them talk.

"You have been a curse on my family," the man said.

"I have tried my best," said the woman.

"If this new baby turns out to be yet another girl, I'm packing up and leaving."

"Fine, because I'm not going to have another."

"I'm sick of your nonsense."

"I'm sick of trying to have a son."

"I'm sick of having so many daughters."

And the six little girls stared open-mouthed and sad-eyed at their parents.

Oh dear! Their little baby wasn't going to be very happy where she was not welcome, decided Sparkling Gem, and she hurried away with the King and servant hurrying behind her.

And so it went on. The search for a good home for the baby angel continued. The poor angels were now hot, hungry and very tired.

"All we want is a home with some comfort and happiness. Where the parents are good and kind and the children are good playmates. Is that really too much to ask for?"

Just then, a mynah bird was passing by. She heard the angels' sad talk. She perched on a branch just above their heads and asked them what the matter was. They told her the whole sad story.

"Mynah bird, you know the earth better than we do, can you not help us find a home where there is enough food to eat? Can you not tell us of a family which has friendly children with parents who look after them with love and kindness?"

After a moment's thought, the mynah bird jumped up and down in excitement. "Yes, I have it, I know a family which just fits this description," she sang. Eagerly the angels followed her, hoping that their search was finally over.

The mynah led them to an old, crumbling house. The gardens were tall with weeds and empty holes gaped where the windows should have been, making the house look like a long-toothed, eyeless creature. The King and Queen looked at each other, worried, but the mynah just flew straight through one of the windows and beckoned to them to follow.

Inside, they could hear the sounds of squealing as if many newborns spoke together. Looking in, the angels saw two cats and around them rolled many balls of fluffy wool. But there was not a human soul in sight.

"What's this?" Quicksilver asked the bird.

"Just the family you seek," was her reply, "the parents look after their young with love and affection, and the brothers and sisters play all day long, with never a quarrel between them."

"But, but they're cats!" cried the Queen.

"Oh?" said the mynah bird, surprised, "cats won't do?"

"How can an angel who looks like a human be brought up by cats?" asked old Zamroo, annoyed.

"Sorry," said the bird, "you said they should be good and kind and friendly and have enough to eat. You never said that they should be human."

The King was about to say something rude to the bird, but the Queen quickly thanked her for taking the trouble and asked if she knew any human families which would fit this description. Once again the bird thought and thought and thought. Finally she said that she would have to think some more.

"If only she had wings, she could have come to live in my nest. I would look after her very well."

"If she had wings, we wouldn't have had any trouble in the first place," said the King, almost shouting.

Well, the bird thought hard, harder and hardest. She tucked her head under her wing and thought some more. Old Zamroo whispered something to the King, which made him pale with worry.

"We must hurry, the angels will be angry when they find us gone. Who knows, they may follow us down to earth to complete the task that they have set their minds on…"

It was true. They were running out of time. They must find Princess Chutki a new home soon.

Before it was too late. Way, way too late.

The bird finally took her head out from under her wing. "I must fly away for a little while. I have some choices, but I must be sure."

"Oh Mynah, please hurry, please hurry," the angels begged. So without further thought or delay, the bird winged away, leaving the group of three angels weary with worry and travel.

BLACK RAIN WILD RAIN STORM

THE sky suddenly darkened with clouds and it looked as if it would rain. Old Zamroo urged the royal family to take shelter in the cat's broken down old home. Having made sure that they were settled in, he himself stepped out and peered up at the dark, forbidding sky.

"It is just as I feared," he muttered under his breath. The clouds that blackened the sky's face were not clouds of life-giving rain. "It is the angels of death that gather in evil masses and block out the Sun," said Zamroo to himself. He knew that they were running out of time, the angels were gathering forces. They had learned that the King and Queen had escaped with the defect baby. They felt angry and cheated. Their spies informed them that the royal had come down to earth, and now they were determined to follow them down and kill the wingless baby.

"What can I do? Oh what can I do?" cried the loyal servant as the first drops of black rain began to fall. He saw, from behind the tree where he had hidden, that each black raindrop carried an angry angel. As the drop splashed on to the ground, it shattered, leaving the angel all fury and ready for battle. Old Zamroo of Zamroodpur trembled with fear. He could not remember a worse time in all his long and eventful life. "Never had the angels left Heaven and come down to Earth to seek out one of their own in this way. Never had the King and Queen had to leave their heavenly home in such a rush and for such a terrible reason."

In the meantime, the mynah bird flew like an arrow to the other side of town. She hardly took notice of the rain at first. But when she saw the people come out and wail at the sight of the rain that blackened their streets and homes and dirtied their washing as it hung out to dry, she took a closer look. When she saw the angry angels gathering in knots of bad intention, she knew that she had very little time left. Now, unmindful of the big, black drops that whizzed past her delicate wings, she flew as fast as she could to the home where, she hoped, would lie the answer.

Young Shera stood by his lovely wife Sonu and watched the rain come down. Their home was quiet and peaceful, unlike the raging storm outside.

People ran helter-skelter, grabbing their drying clothes and snatching up their children who had run out to see the black rain. But Shera and Sonu stood absolutely still. Sonu sighed and turned away from the window with tears in her eyes.

"I wish we too had a grubby, muddy baby to bring in out of the rain. Oh Shera, we would wash her and dress her and then, you and I would play with her…" Sonu's eyes lit up as she pretended to pick a little child up and dress her and comb her hair… "Isn't she lovely?" Sonu asked her husband.

Shera did not have the heart to shatter his wife's fantasy, so he played along. He ran up to her, bent down and picked up the pretend baby, high into his arms. He whirled her round and round and cried, "She isn't only lovely, she's an angel. Look at my angel fly – wheeee!" And he spun like a top, with his arms raised, almost believing that he really held his own baby daughter.

And as he twirled, his eye fell on a brown and wet mynah bird that sat on the windowsill. She looked somehow pleased with what she saw.

"Oh look, the poor bird is getting drenched in the black rain," he said and quickly made for the window to let her in. But quick as a flash, the mynah bird shot off in the opposite direction, back into the filthy rain, unmindful of anything else. She knew that she had found the perfect home. But she also knew that she had very little time left. She knew too, that the journey would be a dangerous one for the royal family. How was she to get them clear across town, when the streets were black with a fury of angels out for blood?

A loud clap of thunder and a streak of flashing lightning blinded the bird and she crashed into a low branch of a tree. She felt a tearing in her right wing. Then, try as she might to fly on, she just fluttered uselessly to the ground. She hit the pavement and felt herself pushed and shoved by

angels left, right and center.

"We must find them!" they shouted.

"We must kill the princess!"

The bird lay flat on the ground, one wing stretched painfully out at her side. She struggled to her feet and tried to fly off, knowing that every precious moment's delay could cost the princess her life. She struggled and she tried to fly, but with a cry of dismay she realized that her wing was broken. She could no longer fly! Trembling with wet and fear, the mynah bird looked around for some way out, some relief. Instead, she saw the angels forming a large black mass on the soggy ground. Thick, like some foul ooze of muck, heaved the puddle of angels. Then, one amongst them flew up onto a rock and here he began to speak.

"It is time now, fellow angels, to gather together and put an end to the wicked princess who has dared to make a wingless entry into the pure and beautiful land of angels. This new princess must never be allowed to grow up. Imagine the shame if she becomes our queen…"

"Shame! Shame!" shouted the angels in one voice.

Their leader seemed to grow inches taller before them, his voice deepening to a manly baritone. He was a wicked malcontent named WB King, called WB for short. But no one knew that his full name was WoodBee King and that he was an angel determined to overthrow the rulers and appoint himself as King, his wife Musn'tsayalot as his silent ever-obedient Queen, and Itchybottom, his precious son as the crown prince. WB saw his best chance now. The perfect opportunity had presented itself and he was going to make full use of it. He could already feel the weight of the crown on his head, the gown on his shoulder, the diamond throne under

SCRATCH!
SCRATCH!

his also itchy bottom. He must complete the job soon now. So he spoke in his newly deepened voice and most slithery convincing tones.

"It is most important," shouted WB, now in a voice of growing confidence, "that we track down the escaped royals as quickly as possible and put an end to this horrible nightmare. It is only once the job is done that goodness and purity will return to our beautiful homeland."

"Find them! Find them!" shouted the crowd, their voices thick with greed and hate.

And all this while. the poor mynah bird tried to pull her wing in and carry out her job immediately. But she fluttered in vain in the rain; the broken wing would not obey.

"But how do we find them?" shouted a voice. Their leader had already made the plan.

"We divide into groups – one to go North, the next South, the third East and the last West. Each group will have a leader who will report back to me."

"Who will be the leaders?" "I will select them from the Chosen Few, of course!" Angel WoodBee King snapped, pointing to some of the athletic types amongst the Chosen Few. They took off their capes and showed their muscles off to the rest. The flabby fat angels tried desperately to pull in their loose, hanging stomachs. Then one of them shouted...

"But what if the King and Queen resist and refuse to give up their baby ?"

The leader said in a hard and cruel voice... "Then we will have no choice but to kill them too!"

The crowd gasped and drew back in horror. Killing the baby princess was one thing. They knew nothing about her. If she had done nothing to harm them, she had never done anything to please them either. But the

King and Queen had always been just and fair. They had always settled the
problems of their land peacefully; they had helped those in trouble and had
always given generous gifts for every birth and wedding. How then, were
they to kill those who had shown them nothing but goodness? The rebel
leader could see that the crowd had not liked his words. He also knew that
he wanted the royals killed. He knew full well that the parents would never
give up the baby and would do everything in their power to save her. He
hoped and prayed that they would. For then the angels would have no
choice but to kill the king and queen. How clear and easy, then, would be
path to the throne. How wonderful it would be to crown oneself King. Oh
then, he would not waste money on gifts and things. No! He would keep it
all to himself. The riches, the food, all the good things that came with being
King of the Heavens would be his and only his (oh, and his son's, of course).
But first, yes first, he must convince the gathered angels to kill their King
and Queen for refusing to give up the Baby in Question.

And now he began to play with their minds. "Think, my friends, think,"
his slimy voice oozed, "does it not make you wonder why the King and
Queen had this wingless creature they dare to call a princess?
Why did it happen to them, and not to you,
or you, or you?" he
pointed into the
crowd, planting

little seeds of doubt with his jabbing finger. And in their fertile minds, the seeds began to sprout. The leader turned on the heat in his voice to provide better conditions for the seeds to take root.

"Could it be, my angel friends, that the K and Q are not quite the angels they say they are?" He dropped his voice to a snaky whisper. He opened his eyes wide as though the thought had just occurred to him, although, in truth, it had been hatching in his evil brain like a rotten egg ever since Princess Chutki had been born. "You don't suppose, brothers and sisters..." he hesitated, stopped, shook his head in confused horror. Every angel's neck craned forward, waiting breathlessly. What could he be thinking? But WB King said nothing, just clapped a clawed hand over his mouth as though the words were too dreadful to bring out into the open.

"What?!" one voice from the crowd shouted out unable to take the tension any more. "What, what?!" more voices shouted out.

And with a great show of the pain it was causing him to give voice to the dreadful suggestion, the leader spoke. "You don't suppose, brothers and sisters, that King Quicksilver and Queen Sparkling Gem are only hu-hu-humans – ordinary humans pretending to be pure, pretending to be one of us?" And now, with great tears that would have put any self-respecting crocodile to shame, the leader watered the plants of doubt that were by this time fruiting and flowering all over the place. (Although I wouldn't really suggest that you eat these fruits for they taste rather bitter, nor decorate your hair with these flowers, for you would become instantly bald!)

It started with a nod here and a nod there. But soon the angels were convinced. The King and Queen must be human, or at least partly human, themselves. It must be their fault that they had had a

Every angel's neck craned forward

rotten baby. Yes, yes, they murmured amongst themselves, their King and Queen must die along with the baby princess. There was no other way to bring purity back to heaven.

The rebel leader smiled an evil smile and began to divide his followers into groups. The injured mynah bird knew that – broken wing, or not – she must make her move now. Now or never. Ever again. She realized now that bringing the royals out of hiding to walk through a town raging with Angels would mean certain death. But what else? How else... wondered the bird. Painfully she gathered her strength and, with an effort that would normally have been impossible, the bird took to the air. Flying on just one wing.

This time she flew in the opposite direction. Back from where she had just come. "If I cannot bring the baby to her new parents, I must take the parents to the baby." That was the only way. Shera and Sonu would have to be convinced that the answer to all their prayers lay on the other side of town. Somehow the bird would have to persuade the young couple to leave their home and follow her, through the blackened streets to an old, crumbling house and accept the angel baby as their own.

NEW CROWN OF THE KING OF ALL HEAVEN...

HEH! HEH! HEH!

...WATERED THE PLANTS OF DOUBT...

These thoughts made the bird fly along, forgetting the pain and rain. She didn't know how she would tell the humans a word of all her plans. But she did know that it had to be done. And fast.

And all this while, King Quicksilver sat with the Queen, the baby playing happily between them. Zamroo of Zamoordpur kept glancing anxiously at the sky. Hoping to catch sight of the bird. "What can be taking her so long?" he wondered anxiously to himself. "Has she given up and gone back to her own nest? Or have the angels caught her? If they beat her up, then she will surely talk. Then they will have no problem in discovering our secret hiding place. We will be trapped like rats. Oh! What a fate for the rulers of the mighty heavens to face," thought the old angel, growing more agitated with every passing second.

The King noticed this, left his Queen to rock the baby to sleep, and joined his loyal servant at the window. He put a comforting hand on Zamroo's shoulder and said, "I am sure she will be back soon with good news…"

But his words dried up as he saw the angry mob of angels, armed with pointed spears, flashing knives and sharp arrows. They were headed directly towards the house.

"Oh, that wretched bird!" moaned Zamroo. "She has betrayed us and has led the mob to our door. I will wring her neck if I ever get the chance!"

The mob was baying, like hounds baying for blood. The Queen's eyes grew wild with worry. "Oh Quicksilver, Zamroo, what do we do, what do we do? Save my baby. Someone save my baby!" she sobbed.

"Mewmewmewmewmew" went the mother and father cat.

"Mewmewmewmewmew give us your baby, we'll hide her. Yes we will."

The cats gathered the kittens round them under their bellies as if to shelter them from the storm. The mob of angels was already at the door. Without waiting another moment, Princess Chutki was placed on the floor amongst the kittens. They huddled up over her, and the parents covered her up with their woolly fur.

The angels outside were breaking down the doors and windows. "Quick, hide!" cried Zamroo.

The doors and windows gave in with a splintering crash. And then, the mob was upon them. "Up here," whispered the King, turning into smoke and wafting up the chimney. The Queen could not bear to leave her baby when the mob came. She turned herself into a tiny flea and hid between the tomcat's toes. Zamroo turned into specks of dust and scattered himself.

The Queen is now a flea-in' queen...

A BABYLESS HOME AND A HOMELESS BABY

THE mynah bird flew, with all her strength and courage. She flew single-winged, through the gloomy sky, with just one thought in mind. How she would manage to do what she must, she did not know. But that she must, she was sure.

The house, when she reached it was locked and barred. The windows shut tight against the storm. The bird flew from window to window until she could see the young couple as they sat by a fire in the kitchen and sipped their tea.

Now, the mynah frantically pecked, scratched and fluttered at the window until she had succeeded in attracting their attention.

"Oh, look at that poor bird. It seems to have hurt itself."

"It also looks as if it's trying to get in!" At last, the window was opened and the exhausted bird tumbled in. Sonu lifted her tenderly in her hands as Shera fetched a soft cloth to wrap her in. Tired as she was, however, the brave bird could not allow herself the luxury of being cared for. She fluttered out of Sonu's hands, back to the window. She tried to tell them that she wanted them to follow. But, "she must be frightened of us," said Shera, backing away from the window. "Let's move away so she's not forced out into the rain."

This was the last thing that the bird wanted. She fluttered straight back into Sonu's hands, lay there panting a moment, before flying to the window again. The humans were puzzled. "How odd!" she said. "Do you think she's trying to tell us something?" said Shera.

This time the bird landed on Shera's shoulder, trying to tell him that his guess was right. With the bird still on his shoulder, he walked to the window. Promptly, the bird flew out and landed on the ground, took a few steps forward, then looked back, hoping that they would understand that she wanted them to follow her.

"Do you think she wants us to follow her?" asked Sonu, joining her husband at the window.

"I think you're right," he agreed. And without further delay, they locked up their home, took two umbrellas to protect themselves from the rain, and stepped out.

The bird chirruped in relief and hopped forward, but Shera scooped her up, off the soggy ground saying, "Don't fret, little one, and don't tire yourself anymore. We'll follow you wherever you want us to go, just point out the way with your beak, we'll understand."

The mynah chirruped her thanks and led them along. At last she was going to save the beautiful Princess Chutki. At last she would be of some greater use than the eating and sleeping that had filled her days all this time. She fluffed up her brown, black and white feathers, pleased with the difficult task she had accomplished.

"STOP!" shouted a voice, "HALT!" Shera and Sonu stopped. Peeping out from between Shera's fingers, the bird saw a posse of uniformed gunmen stand in their way.

"What are you carrying in your hands? Put it down so we can examine it."

"But, it's nothing," said Sonu, "just a poor bird with a broken wing."

"PUT IT DOWN!" thundered the leader, and the heavens thundered in echoed anger.

Shera placed the bird gently on the ground. But the men in uniform were not so gentle. One of them poked the bird with the barrel of his gun. He rolled her over onto her back and poked her broken wing.

"Stop that," cried Sonu, bending down to pick her up.

"STAY BACK!" the men thundered together as lightning lit up the sky. The bird, lying flat on her back, now noticed that the feet of these men did not quite touch the ground. They sort of floated just above the earth. So, these were not men, but the angels disguised as men.

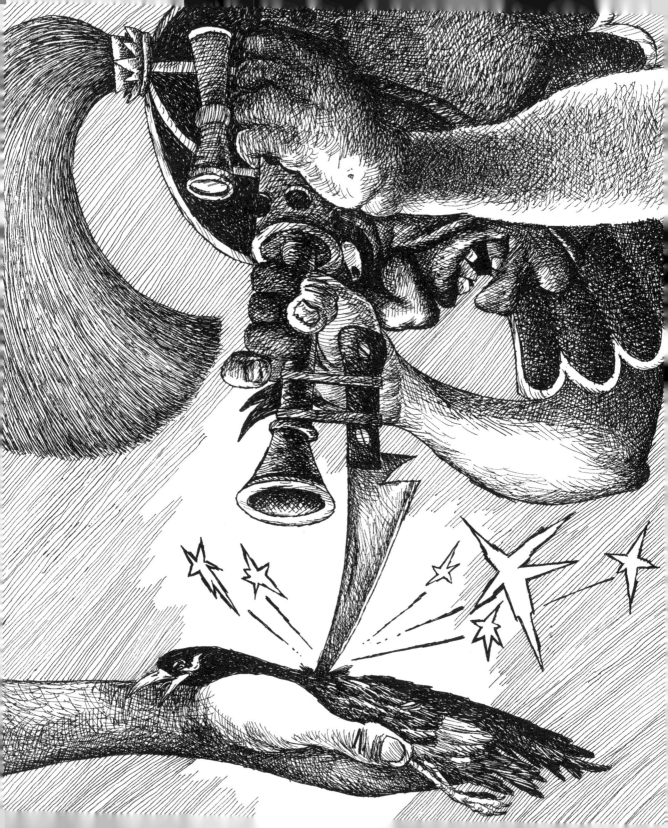

"It's nothing, just a sick and dying bird," muttered the leader, giving one more jab at the broken wing in disgust. The bird trembled with pain.

Shera picked the mynah up again and they were about to walk away, when one of the men said, "Hey, isn't this the same bird that lay on the ground when our plans were being drawn up by our leader?"

"Could be, but what difference does it make? It's only a bird with a broken wing."

"True, but... but how has it come so far with a broken wing? And why?"

"You think it may have something to do with what we seek?"

"Hey you, where did you get this bird?"

"Er----," said Shera immediately guessing that the bird's strange behaviour must have something to do with whatever it was those men were looking for. "Er – this bird was brought to us by a friend, sir!"

"You see, all our friends know that we care for sick birds, so they bring them to us whenever they find one," Sonu added, catching on fast.

"And where are you taking it now, in this storm?"

"To a doctor who will tend to its injuries…"

"...Or else, it will die." The tears in Sonu's eyes were real, for she was touched by the little bird's strength and courage in protecting whatever it was that she was trying to protect. She wondered, too, why she and Shera had been chosen as a part of this plan.

The uniformed men stomped their feet in disappointment, but had to let the couple go.

"I'm tired," grumbled one.

"Let's sit down at some restaurant and have a bite to eat," suggested the other, smacking his rubbery lips.

"March on, march on!" their leader commanded, pulling their noses.

"The Princess must be found. Come on, hop to it." And off they marched shouting, "Left, right! Left, right! Pajama dhila, topi tight!"

DUST AND SMOKE AND FLEAS

MEANWHILE, back at the old house, when the maddened mob broke down the door, they found very little. A dusty old house, that was falling to pieces and was occupied only by a cat family. The angry angels rushed up the stairs and down the stairs, they tore cupboards, which turned out to be occupied only by spiders and lizards. They stamped and jumped about so hard that they stirred up the dust till it tickled their nostrils and made them sneeze. They peered up the chimney but the smoke got into their eyes and made them cry.

"Boo! Hoo! Hoo!
Achoo Achoo!"

At last, teary-eyed, runny-nosed but empty-handed, they started to leave. One of them, just out of angry disappointment, decided to kick the cats.

"Meeworrr," snorted the tomcat, showing his sharp teeth and nails but not moving an inch. The angel jumped back in startled fear and ran for the door. But here he stopped. He grabbed another angel by the arm. "Something strange…" he whispered, "here, look," and he kicked the cat again. This time both the adult cats showed their teeth and claws. The hair on their shoulders stood straight up. But they didn't move from their kittens.

"I don't see anything strange," said the second angel. "Come on, let's go!"

"No wait," said the first. "Don't you think it odd that they don't get up and run when they're kicked?"

"They've got kittens, can't you see? How can they run? Now be an angel, stop troubling the poor cats and let's get out of this place."

"You go, if you want. I say there's something strange, I'm going to take a look and see if these cats are trying to hide something," and he bent down and began to pick the kittens up one by one! The cats bunched up together, trying hard to cover Princess Chutki.

"Hey!" shouted the angel, making his friend stop at the door. But suddenly, Dust kicked up. Smoke came billowing out from the old chimney with such force that it blinded the angel's eyes. He was hit on the head by a flying brick when his

hand was just inches away from the princess's face. Flea jumped out of the cat's fur and bit the prying hand. Hard.

"Ow!" yelped the angel, "Ow! Ouch! Dirty, filthy cats." He looked at his hand through teary eyes and saw a tiny, tiny flea biting away at his hand.

"Filthy, dirty, flea-ridden cats!" cried the angel, squashing the flea with the other hand and flicking it off.

"I told you, there's nothing here," said the angel's friend, "now come on before our leader finds us dilly-dallying here and punishes us!" He took the dusty, smoky, flea-bitten angel by the hand and led him away, banging the door behind him like a bad boy.

When all was quiet and still once again, the king re-materialized himself from the smoke. The dust gathered itself up to become old Zamroo. But where was Queen Sparkling Gem?

Frantically, the two angels and the two adult cats searched and called, called and searched. But there was no reply…

There was, instead, a knock on the door. Peeping out, old Zamroo saw with relief that it was not the angry angels, but the mynah bird, back once again with a human couple. He opened the door.

"Come in," he said, "but step no further than in."

"Why?"

"We can't find the Queen. Obviously she turned herself into something."

"But we don't know why she isn't turning back into herself."

Just then Princess Chutki, tired of lying still on the floor, giggled out loud as the kitten's fur tickled her.

"Oh my, what a beautiful baby!" cried Sonu, and almost rushed over to pick her up. But Quicksilver quickly held her back.

"You might step on my wife. Be careful please. You see, we all had to transform ourselves into something or the other to hide from the Angel Army that came snooping here a little while back. Now that the danger's past, we've all assumed our old forms again, but not Queen Sparkling Gem, my wife. Something must be wrong with her, she could be anywhere around here, too tiny for us to see. So please," he cautioned, "don't step anywhere, for you could be stepping on my darling wife." Instead, he flew over to his daughter, picked her up, and placed her in the welcoming, loving arms of Sonu. The baby smiled up and gurgled, as Sonu hugged her and whispered, "I wish you were mine!"

"She's yours," whispered a tiny, tiny voice.

"Who said that?" asked Sonu puzzled.

"Said what?" asked the others.

"It's the Queen, the baby's mother," came the tiny, tiny voice again.

"It's – It's the Queen!" said Sonu amazed.

"But where is she?" asked the others.

The mynah bird, with eyes that were used to spotting and hunting tiny insects, made out the small struggling body of a flea, squirming amongst the baby's curly hair.

The King picked the flea up. Sure enough,

it was his wife. She was hurt. She was weak. Too hurt and weak to turn herself back into an angel at the moment. But yet, she was happy.

She sighed in a tired but happy voice, "My baby has found a kind and wonderful mother!"

"She is yours," said King Quicksilver, placing his hand on the young couple. "Love her and treasure her and treat her well. She must live like an angel."

"She will, she will be our princess, our angel. She will want for nothing," promised Shera and Sonu in one voice.

The cats were thanked by the royal angels. The mynah bird was kissed by the King. And her broken wing mended at once. Shera and Sonu were blessed with the baby that they had always yearned for.

"And now we must leave," said the King, holding his Queen Flea carefully. They kissed their beautiful daughter one last time and then, with the faithful old Zamroo of Zamroodpur as company, the royals returned to their home in Heaven.

Life on Earth

A ND so it was that the Princess (who could not be a princess) and a young couple (who could not have a child of their own) found each other.

The new parents loved and adored their new daughter. And Chutki, as she was now plainly called, never gave her parents a moment's pain or worry or sadness.

After the King, Queen and Zamroo had left, Shera and Sonu waited, hoping that the path would soon be clear for them to carry their daughter back home. The father cat decided to go out to have a look, but he came in soon, saying that there was danger yet. "Perhaps when it is dark," thought Shera. But long after the sun had set and the moon had risen, the angels stormed non-stop, tormenting the people of the town, waking them up and barging into homes in search of the Disappeared Baby.

Even days later, after the storm had quietened, long after the streets had dried, even after most of the angels had returned to their land of diamonds and silver, there were still some groups of uniformed angels to be seen, marching up and down the streets. They would look suspiciously

..Perhaps when it is dark..

at almost everything, but most especially, they would closely examine any little baby that happened to be out.

So Shera and Sonu knew that they could not bring Chutki out to make the journey across town.

"Let's move into this house," said Sonu, "if the cats don't mind sharing their home?" She stroked the mother cat, while the cat ran her body liquidlike about the young woman's legs.

"She doesn't seem to mind," laughed Shera, "and look, neither do they!" He pointed at the kittens as they played with Chutki who squealed with delight.

And so it was that Shera and Sonu moved out of their perfect, clean and empty home to the run-down, crumbling one that seemed always full of bubbling laughter.

The mynah bird, too, decided to build a new nest in the big peepul tree that stood guard over the tumbling walls and weeds of the house, from where the bird watched all day long, especially when Chutki and the kittens were playing in the garden. Whenever a troop of searching angels approached, the bird would flutter down and chirp and chirrup until the child was well hidden.

Shera and Sonu worked hard and happily, putting back windows, repairing the chimney, weeding the big, old garden.

Room by room, the house was once again shining and bright. What a relief it was to have a house busy with laughter. Actually Chutki, being born of royalty, was a very neat baby, swiftly potty-training herself. But Sonu and Shera, her new parents, would have none of that. Oh no, they made her pull her toys out of drawers if she put them away and scatter them up and down the stairs and all over the place. Once, Shera even upturned the potty all over the floor, but Sonu thought that that was going too far. There were still some rooms left unopened and untended but they decided that they didn't need more space and they were as happy as any 'lived-happily-everafter' family in the best fairy tale tradition. Food

wasn't plenty, but it was enough. Sonu was a very inventive cook. She made barfi out of vegetables, digestive biscuits out of books and dosas out of napkins. And they were delicious. And there wasn't much furniture, but there was television and a cable connection. So all in all, life wasn't bad at all.

And every night, from Heaven, King Quicksilver and Queen Sparkling Gem would beam their Beamable Vision earthwards and sigh with pleasure. They knew now that they need not have despaired that longago time when they searched in vain for a perfect home for their imperfect baby. It didn't seem possible then, but now this happy home had everything that a happy baby of a happy age could possibly wish for. King Quicksilver and Queen Sparkling Gem would beam beaming smiles after they switched off their Beamable Vision. Yes, they had made the best choice in the worst circumstances.

And little Chutki had her kitten brothers and sisters to play with. In fact, she always thought she was a cat. She crawled around the floors with them and though her human mother tried to stop her, Chutki always lapped up her milk from a plate instead of drinking it from a glass like U and I. Naturally, the first sounds she made were "Mew! Mew! Mew!" "One day you'll grow a cat's tail if you don't watch out," Sonu would say, playfully tickling the baby's backside. And Chutki did her very best to grow a tail. But like her wings wouldn't grow, neither would her tail.

Shera, as I've never mentioned before, was a Polisher of Things. That was his job. He went from house to house, shop to shop and street to street polishing any dull surface that needed a shine. Tables, chairs, windows, cars, bathrooms, mirrors, shoes and handbags, brass and silver, why, even bald heads. He applied his skill along with his polish and cloth. Yes indeed, he was the best Polisher of Things.

WHY EVEN Bald HEH! HEH! HEADS.

Now, on his visits to people's homes and shops, he heard the people complain,

"Where have these uniformed men come from?"

"What do they want from us?"

"And from our babies?"

"My baby is woken up and examined all the time!"

"Yes, mine too. He was so annoyed, that he bit the finger of one of the men as he was being checked out."

"Ha! Ha! Ha! Serves them right."

"Oh, I don't know, this fellow went into such a fit of rage that he broke two windows on his way out."

Or,

"They walk in here and help themselves to whatever they like."

"Never paying."

"Never even asking."

"And leaving mud all over the floors besides."

"Whatever are they after?"

Then, of course, there came a time when the angels' boots and brass-buckled belts dulled and lost their gloss. And we couldn't have that with such perfect examples of angeldom. So, of course, the Polisher of Things was sent for. And, of course, he had to go even though he knew that they would not pay him for the price of his polish, let alone his labour.

Sure enough, morning to night, poor Shera worked, polishing belts, shoes, badges and even toenails. He polished till his back ached and his fingers couldn't move any more. But still the polishing never ended.

"Be back again tomorrow," they commanded. Tired, weary, but with empty pockets, Shera returned home.

"Doesn't matter," soothed Sonu, "we have enough food for a day or two."

The next day and the next, Shera reported to work and everyday more and more things were found for him to polish. Cars and motorbikes stolen from humans. Watches and rings, buttons and jewelry. It went on and on. First they assured him that it was just for a day or two. But soon, it became a week or two and then a month or two. Not only was money running low, but so were Shera's spirits and, of course, the food supplies. Surely, he thought, they've got to run out of things that need polishing. But that was not to be.

For one day, WB King decided that the streets of the town, upon which the angels must walk, should be polished until they shone like the silver streets back home! Now even for the best Polisher of Things, turning roads as black as cobras into streets of silver was asking for too much. Especially when he had not had much to eat for two or three days and had worked himself to the bone. Down on his hands and knees, under the hot sun, poor Shera scrubbed and polished till his hands were black and his clothes were black and the streets were blacker than ever. But for all this efforts, all he ever got were abuses and no money at all.

Their kitchen was now empty and bare. The cats caught mice and brought them to Sonu and the mynah brought insects and worms, but of course, the humans could not eat them, hungry as they were.

Now, while there were a lot of very special things that Sonu could do awfully well, they weren't exactly the kind of things that got you a lot of money. For instance, she was very good at talking backwards. So she could say 'sdrawkcab' for 'backwards' as easily as you can say your own name.

And she could say whole nursery rhymes backwards so that

Mary had a little lamb

sounded like

Bmal elttil a dah yram

and *Malayalam*

sounded like, well, *Malayalam.*

Quite a talent, but no office or restaurant or bank would really need such a person.

The other thing she was good at was singing at such a high pitch that she could break glass with her voice, without even touching it once! But jobs for glass-shatterers were very few, especially now, when the angel army was busy breaking things all over the place. So though she searched and searched for a job until she was quite, quite tired and quite, quite hungry, she was unable to find anything suitable. And all the while, poor Shera, the famous Polisher of Things polished the roads to blackness instead of silverness and was bullied, beaten and unpaid for all his efforts.

RECONCILIATION in HEAVEN

NOW you may think that this would be as good a time as any for the King and Queen of Angels to do some magic here and there and provide their daughter with a magic pot which cooked food when you said some magic words, or a purse which never emptied. Or at the very least, they would turn the streets silver for Shera. That's what should happen in any good fairy tale. But not in this one – you see, it couldn't. *They* couldn't. The parents, I mean. They could provide no magic for their daughter or her new parents for they knew how dangerous that could be. If the angel army detected any hint of magic as it travelled all the way from heaven to earth, then all would be lost. Of course it pained the King and Queen (who, by the way, was still flea-formed because she had not the strength or will to become an angel again) to see how unangelically their subjects were behaving. They felt guilty too, for they knew that it was all because of them that the angels had gone to earth in the first place. They also worried about Chutki, although she blossomed and bloomed like a prize rose in spite of the difficulties her family faced.

And so they decided to call a meeting of the angels in heaven and sort matters out with them. As the angels gathered in the land of diamonds and silver, those on earth knew that they too must go to attend the meeting. They left enough spies, however, to keep a watch out for the missing baby.

EAR TO THE GROUND

They left enough spies...

59

"Fellow angels," began the King, "things have happened in our land of goodness and purity which are neither good, nor pure…"

"But we didn't start it, you did," shouted Angel WoodBee King who was sorely disappointed that his best plans had failed.

"We don't know why we had a wingless baby," admitted the King, getting straight to the point. "We would have loved to have had a baby who was perfect – who wouldn't? But, now here's the point," his voice dropped, softened. "We loved our imperfect baby perfectly. Wings or no wings, she was beautiful, wonderful, cheerful and loving. Are wings the only sign of being an angel? Is that all that symbolizes or identifies an angel? Would it have been quite alright if she'd had wings but, say, no nose, or three eyes?

WE Didn't Start it, You did!

Would it have been quite alright if she'd had wings, but a black, evil heart?" The King looked hard at the ones he knew had been brewing trouble. They shifted their feet, shifty-eyed.

"But," continued Quicksilver, "we realized that you, our people, were unhappy and as King and Queen it is our duty to do all we can to make our people happy. So, although we loved our precious daughter dearly, we parted with her for your peace of mind, although it fairly broke our hearts to do so. I can only hope you believe us," his voice was liquiding into tears.

It started with a nod here and a nod there. But soon the angels were convinced. Yes, yes, they murmured amongst themselves, the King and Queen must be forgiven.

"And where is the baby now?" demanded WoodBee King, in a desperate last-ditch attempt.

"We have dealt with the baby in the proper way. You need not worry about her anymore."

"Then where is the Queen?" WoodBee demanded yet again. He was sure that she was still on earth with the baby princess. Besides, he could see his grand plans coming apart like some old cloth.

"The Queen, *your* Queen, is broken-hearted, my friend," and once again Quicksilver looked hard at the bullying angel. "It was hard enough for her to turn her back on our baby daughter, as perhaps all you mothers out there can imagine…"

Some mother angels wiped tears of sympathy from their eyes. They suddenly felt very sorry for their Queen.

"BUT," continued the King, "what has hurt her, indeed us, even more, is that you, all of you, could so easily forget everything that we ever did for you. How could you imagine that we would do anything

SNIFF! SNIFF! SNIFF! SNIFF!

to harm our land? How could you think that we would put our happiness above yours? Queen Sparkling Gem lies in bed, too broken-hearted to eat or sleep. Too saddened to sparkle. And there she will lie until someday something can make her happy once again."

The angels hung their heads, ashamed. Soon all was right with the heavens again except, of course, that the Queen pined, flea-formed, for her wingless daughter.

Back on earth, things were slowly returning to normal. The word spread amongst the angel spies who had been left behind. Moonbeams beamed the King's moving speech worldwide. They also carried urgent messages from their families. Messages like:

BABY TWINS BORN - COME BACK SOON

MOTHER SERIOUS - RETURN HOME IMMEDIATELY

ALL SINS FORGIVEN AND FORGOTTEN - PLEASE RETURN

or, even just

YOU'VE FAILED YOUR EXAMS AGAIN - GET BACK NOW!

(signed FATHER + HEADMASTER)

So all of them took the nearest moonbeam and shot back home. Well, almost all, except, I must tell you, the last one, who had fallen in love with a trapeze artist. He ripped his own angelness off when no one was looking and ran off to become a very successful magician in a magic-and-trapeze circus, but that's another story.

Finally, Shera could stop polishing streets and get back to polishing more usual things and most of all earning money for it. Sonu, too, soon found an excellent and exciting profession. She was hired by a record company to sing well-known songs backwards. She was a great hit amongst the people, and her records, tapes and CDs began to sell like hot cakes. She also was a good cook, remember, and baked a lot, so that her hot cakes sold like records, tapes and CDs.

So they were now really like a 'lived-happily-everafter' family. Family, fame, fortune and fun were rolled into one wonderful place.

And if you think that's the end of this tale, you're mistaken, for this is a fairly weird fairy tale.

TRUTH TIME

TIME passed, as it always does. Things changed, as they tend to do. Some for the better, some for the worse. Children grew up and became adults, as they unfortunately usually do. Even some adults grew down and became children again, but they're not part of this story. No.

And I'm sure that you're *dying* to know what happened to Chutki and all her friends, and both her families. (*Well, even if you're not dying to know, I'm sure you want to finish this book, so, okay, here's the very last chapter.*)

So, let's fast-forward a bit, to sometime in the present. When Chutki had started, not just to mew, but also to speak in the language of her parents. Actually, she also had a fine singing voice like her mother, although, being against child labour and all that, they hadn't got her into earning money out of her voice as yet.

Meanwhile, her earth family was going from strength to strength. Money was finally no problem. For the Polisher of Things was a success at his polishing, just as he had always been. The Backward Singer, on the other hand, was a HUGE success, putting all the major singers of the time out of business. Cycle Traction would be booed off stage no matter how well he danced and sang. Sons of Noses and Delayed Mehndi could do no better than to provide back-up vocals for the Backward Singer.

In short, all was Right with the World as Chutki sat on a branch with the mynah who was giving the child lessons. You see, the cat taught Chutki the Ground Rules while the mynah taught her Sky Rules. They were in the process of trying to find a wise fish to teach their pupil the Water Rules. "It'll be difficult, of course," sneered the cat cattily, "for fish are only fishy, never wise."

But the Point is that the mynah now sat her pupil down on a branch to teach her the Rules of Weather Watching.

"When there are fluffy, white clouds and plenty of blue sky, it means the weather will be fine. Chutki, are you paying attention?" scolded Mynah, noticing the faraway look on the girl's face. "Yes, yes," she mumbled, dreamily, obviously paying no attention at all.

Crossly Mynah said, "I could fall off this branch at this very moment and crack my skull open, and what would you say?"

"That would be lovely," sighed the girl dreamily.

"...And then I'd die of a broken skull and heart and what would you say then?" snapped the bird, stabbing Chutki with her beak.

66

"Huh? Oh… Oh…, I… I'd say it was… er… going to r-rain?" stammered the red-faced girl, with not a clue as to what she should be saying. Seeing the anger on her teacher's face, Chutki picked her up tenderly in her hands, and kissed her gently on the beak.

"Stop it, put me down at once. If all children picked their teachers up into their laps and kissed them, think of what would happen in the world…"

"I think that it would be just lovely…" sighed the girl, picturing hundreds of angry teachers being kissed in their students' laps. She smoothened the bird's ruffled feathers. Of course it worked. Like it did every time.

"Alright, alright," said the teacher, settling comfortably into her student's lap. "So tell me, what were you really thinking of this time?"

"Mynah, please, please, please can you teach me to fly? Please…?"

"Oh Chutki, not that again. You know that I can't teach you to fly."

"But why not? Why not? Why not?!" shouted Chutki, and then she burst into tears. "It's not fair! You teach your own children to fly. But you don't teach me. I know you don't love me, that's why…"

She sobbed. The bird sighed. They'd been through all this before, but the girl just refused to be reasonable and understand.

"Oh Chutki, why can't you be reasonable and understand, you-can-not-fly!!"

"Why not?"

"Because you don't have wings, that's why."

"But why not? It's not fair."

"If you had wings," muttered the bird under her breath, "you wouldn't even be here."

"Why not?"

"Oh nothing, nothing."

"No, tell me, please, tell me what you were saying."

"Chutki, please, it's a long story and... and I'm tired. Please, go now. I need to be alone."

But have you ever known a child to give up on the chance of a story so easily?

"Please, please, please, please, please

Oh, "   "   "   "   "

Oh, mynah, "   "   "   "

I'll do ANYTHING you EVER tell me to.

Please, please, please, please, please

Oh "   "   "   "   "

P-L-E-E-E-E-E-E-E-E-E-E-E-E-
ZZZZZZZZZZZZZZZZZZZZZZ!!!!!!"

So, although the mynah didn't want to... Although she knew she really shouldn't... Although she knew that Shera and Sonu would probably be really angry with her, although she knew that she'd be really, really sorry later, the mynah had no other choice, but to open her beak and spill the beans about where Chutki had come from.

Chutki's eyes grew wider and wider as the bird revealed her story. When, at last, it was over, the little girl sat quietly, letting it all sink in.

"I wonder, is that why I'm always longing to fly, d'you think? Because I should have been able to?" asked the little girl in a little girl voice.

"I don't know, but I've thought about that too, quite often," replied the bird, wishing she had held her tongue, yet knowing that Truth Time comes, sooner or later. The girl sat quietly for some more time, then spoke as if from a faraway place.

"An an... Angel?... a princess? B-but Mynah, I'm so, I'm so ordinary. So plain."

"No, you're special, you're the most wonderful child I've ever had the pleasure of knowing."

"Me, special?" laughed the girl, "what's so special about me my dear, dear teacher?"

"Your heart is pure, your thoughts are good, you are as innocent as a child should be, yet as wise as any old grandfather could ever hope to be. You are the two sides of any coin. Perfect, shining."

"But is that enough to be the daughter of the King and Queen of the Heavens? Is that enough for me to have become the ruler of the angels, when the time came, even if I had been born with wings?"

"I'm just a bird. I'm not sure about Grand Things. But one thing I do know, there could be no better ruler than you, whether up there or down here. That I do know for sure."

"And yet... And yet my parents chose to give me away..." said Chutki in a small voice, tears spilling out of her eyes and trembling on her eye-lashes. The bird wiped the tears away with her silken feathers, she rubbed her soft head against the girl's neck and explained.

"I know how hard they struggled, the dangers they undertook to find the perfect home for you. I know how it broke their hearts when the time came for them to leave you."

And the bird told the child of how the mother had turned herself into a flea to escape detection. How she had bitten the investigating soldier's hand to get him away from the baby. How she had almost lost her life in the effort. And how, when she was leaving her only child behind, she was too broken-hearted to change back to her original form. That she had returned to Heaven in her new avatar as a flea. "For all you know," the mynah concluded, "she may be a flea even today."

Chutki sat, silently soaking in all the new things she had learned about herself. Finally, she sighed, "and all because I could not fly." And she shook her head. As the words left her mouth, her eyes lit up, "…because I could not fly." Her voice rose a little, edged with excitement.

"I could not fly------fly-----fly. Oh Mynah, I have it, I have it don't you see, I have it?"

"No, I don't see," said the mynah, hunching down into herself, for, I think, she could see the idea that was forming itself in the little girl's mind. She could see it, but she didn't like it. No. Not one little bit.

"If I could fly…"

"You CANNOT fly. Chutki, to fly you need wings… you don't have them. If you had wings, you wouldn't be here…"

"But Mynah, I could try. I could learn. I could…"

"No!" shouted the bird in a tear-strained voice.

"Why not?"

"You don't have wings."

"I could make some."

"It won't work."

"I could try."

"No!"

"Why not?"

"It won't work."

"I could try Mynah, I want to…"

"No. It won't work!"

"Oh alright, bird, it won't work, so it won't work. But haven't you always taught me that you never know unless you try? Don't you see, I've got to try?" Now it was the bird's turn to be quiet.

"Me and my big beak. It's all my fault," she finally murmured.

"It's not your fault. I've always wanted to fly, you know that. Perhaps that's because I was always *meant* to fly…"

"Yes, and now that I've told you the truth about your birth, you're going to try and fly. If you fail you'll end up being so disappointed. But if… if by some strange chance you do succeed… OH, I can't bear to think about it," sobbed the poor bird.

"Can't bear to think of me succeeding? Why, bird, that's not fair! What kind of teacher are you?!" The girl was hurt and angry as she jumped down off the tree. "I'm not talking to you."

The bird flew after the stomping girl, "Wait, listen…"

"I'm not talking to you…"

"Alright, don't talk, just listen…"

"No!"

"Please, it's important…"

"No!!"

"It's about your parents."

"Which parents?" the girl stopped abruptly to turn and face her teacher who was flying right next to her. The bird bumped into her ear and fell clumsily to the ground. "Ouch!" The girl sat on the ground next to the fallen teacher.

She picked her up.

"Your earth parents, your sky parents... ooof, I just don't know. What I know is that we all love you so very dearly. All of us. All we want... ever wanted to do... was to protect you from all the harm that surrounded you from the moment of your birth. That's all we've ever wanted – all of us."

"But Mynah, what do you think? Was it so bad that I was born without wings? So bad that the others would have to kill me?"

"No!" the bird exploded in a rush of angry feathers... "Of course not."

"But if a bird were to be born without wings, would you, could you accept her as a bird?"

"A bird without wings," Mynah laughed, "there's no such thing, it could never happen."

"But it did, don't you see, an angel without wings is just as bizarre as a bird without wings. There's no such thing, yet, here I am. So, would the other birds accept such a creature as a bird, tell me?"

Mynah tried hard to think positively. But the truth was that a wingless baby bird would probably have been killed, or, at the very best, allowed to die within hours of its birth. Was it the same with angels? Mynah had never thought of it like this. She'd always blamed the angels for having been mean and small-hearted, yet, would she have behaved in the same way, faced with the same situation? She wasn't so sure anymore.

WHAT'S WRONG?

Just then, the tomcat came up, ready to take Chutki off to her next lesson. But one look at the other two and he knew that something was wrong.

"What's wrong?"

And when he heard that the bird had told the girl about her heavenly origins, he was so angry that he felt, "I could just eat you up."

"It wouldn't do you any good if you did. The truth is out now. And it was always going to be, sooner or later."

So, what was going to happen now? Would Chutki learn to fly? Could she? And what then? Would she fly away forever? Or, more likely, would she try and try and never fly? And what then, would her heart break with disappointment? What was better, that she managed to fly and break their hearts, or didn't, and broke her own? Questions buzzed like annoying flies around their heads. The mother cat joined them and heard what had happened.

And then it was Sonu and Shera who heard the news. The same questions hovered over their heads too. Was it better for her to fly? Fly away? And then, would her family and the other angels accept her, wingless though she still was? Or was it better for her to live with the truth that she was a princess who would never be a queen, an angel on earth who would never fly? Which was better, or rather, which was less worse?

The five of them sat in a worried circle. What they didn't know was that they had formed a circle of love. A circle of magic. So absorbed were they that they scarcely noticed when Chutki came and stood within the magic power of the circle. Her eyes were closed. Her face upturned to her birthhome. Her feet firmly planted on the soil of her homehome. Her arms stretched up. There were no wings, but her arched back seemed ready to spring her into magical lands. Her arms stretched wide high over her head, receiving. She seemed to glow. But not a fierce glow, more like the gentle warmth of a setting sun. Or a dawning one. And then she spoke in a voice of wondrous strength and beauty.

"I am ready," she announced to every one of them and to no one in particular, "I am ready. If you are ready for me."

"Chutki," whispered the cats, the bird and the girl's human parents who completed the magical circle.

"Chutki," whispered her King father and Queen mother in the Heavens.

"Chutki," sang the thousands of angels as they peeped through the clouds, in pink and gold voices of celebration.

"Chutki," the voices were one. The name was one. The Oneness of One. Each one so different. Yet the same. Differences forgotten now. At the wonder that was Chutki.

The three Note children, Bada Note, Chotta Note and little Change glanced away from their TV screens to see the goldening sky more gold, more jewelled than anything they'd ever seen before. "What's happening?" Bada and Chotta whispered in wonder. "I don't know, but I love it!" breathed Change, his smile reflecting the radiance of the magic sky. And they were suddenly richer than they'd ever been before.

And then the earth began to rise up and the sky began to descend. Up and up. Down and down. Higher and higher. Lower and lower. Until Chutki's arms were in Heaven, but her feet were rooted to the ground beneath. The sky blued and the clouds shone with a neverbefore light and beauty. The ground she stood on sprang up with a million flowers, nodding their bright heads in approval.

Runny-nosed children stopped scratching their heads and watched in open-mouthed, open curiosity as the grass sprang green beneath their feet and the sky lowered its glorious head and kissed them. They could not but hold each other's hands to help absorb the beauty of the magic before their very eyes. And they were never poor again.

And still Heaven and Earth stretched towards each other. With longing. With love. Until, at last, Heaven and Earth were joined. And Chutki lay down. Holding onto one with her right hand and the other with her left.

Earth had become Heaven and Heaven, Earth.

Joined forever to those who have always loved her, and also to those who had not, Chutki showed those who cared to see that an angel doesn't need wings to be an angel.

And that is how the Horizon came to be. Joining the two Kingdoms of Princess Chutki, as she took her rightful place in both her homes.

And you can see her even today, looking her most beautiful, adorned in jewelled gold at sunrise and sunset. For she lies there still, making sure that both her homes and all her people live in magic forever.

So, whenever you are lonely, whenever you need a friend, just look far out into the horizon. As far as your eye can see. And you will see her.

Princess Chutki. Princess Horizon. Beautiful. Calm. Forever.

THE
END